Good Night Little Bunny

Written By LaTrell Halcomb
Illustrated By Delly Yusyar Achmadi

The sun is down, the moon is up,
it's time for bed, little one.

It's about time for the little bunny to lay down his furry little head. But first, he must finish his tasty carrots instead.

ext to the carrots were a pair of parrots
that kept asking for him to share it.

Then he hops into his room
and picks up a broom.

He sweeps the trash as quick as a flash.

Then he feeds his goldfish,
whose name is Dash.

Next, it's bath time for little Bunny! Filling the bathtub with warm water and tons of bubbles. Scrub, Scrub, Scrub all over his fury body, making sure he's nice and clean.

The sun is down, the moon is up,
it's almost time for bed, everyone.

After that, he enjoys brushing his teeth. Making them so shiny that you could see your reflection.

It's jammie time! Little Bunny hopped into his closet, saw his rocket, and grabbed his coziest pajamas that he got from the market.

The sun is down, the moon is up, and it's getting closer to bedtime, everyone.

Now, little Bunny wants a bedtime story, so he's searching all over his room for the right book.
He took a second look, and he found The Planet of the Bunny's Book.

The Planet
of
the Bunny's
Book

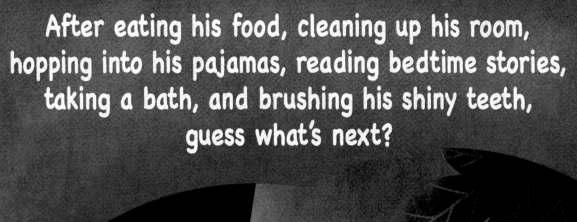

After eating his food, cleaning up his room, hopping into his pajamas, reading bedtime stories, taking a bath, and brushing his shiny teeth, guess what's next?

"It's finally time for bed,"
the bunny's mom and dad said.
They laid a soft pillow under his head and said
"I love you to the moon and back."
Gave him a hug and tucked him in like a Bug in a rug.

As the world is asleep and, in their beds,
"I can't wait until the morning," the little bunny said.

He starts to yawn and snuggle into his bed.
His eyelids began to roll into the back
of his head, when suddenly drool
began to hit the bed.

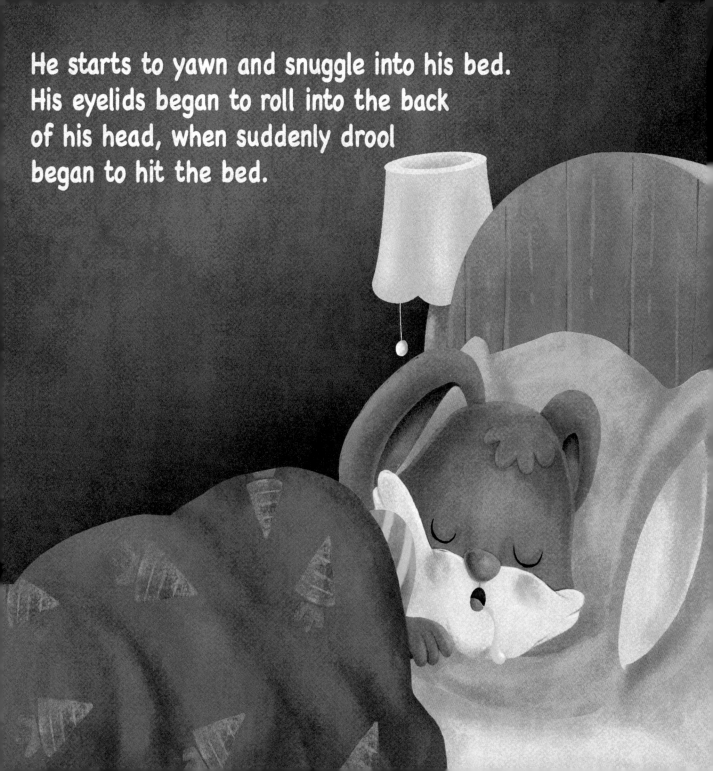

Within seconds, he's snoring and dreaming away, about how tomorrow is going to be a great day!

The sun is down, the moon is up,
it's now time for bed, everyone!

Made in the USA
Columbia, SC
16 February 2023

12196090R00015